Dear mouse friends,
Welcome to the world of

Geronimo Stilton

THE RODENT'S GAZETTE
EDITORIAL STAFF

Geronimo Stilton
A learned and brainy
mouse; editor of
The Rodent's Gazette

Thea Stilton
Geronimo's sister and
special correspondent at
The Rodent's Gazette

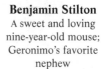

Trap Stilton
An awful joker;
Geronimo's cousin and
owner of the store
Cheap Junk for Less

Benjamin Stilton
A sweet and loving
nine-year-old mouse;
Geronimo's favorite
nephew

Geronimo Stilton

THE GIANT DIAMOND ROBBERY

Scholastic Inc.

Copyright © 2016 by Edizioni Piemme S.p.A., Palazzo Mondadori, Via Mondadori 1, 20090 Segrate, Italy. International Rights © Atlantyca S.p.A. English translation © 2018 by Atlantyca S.p.A.

The publisher does not have any control over and does not assume any responsibility for author or third-party websites or their content.

GERONIMO STILTON names, characters, and related indicia are copyright, trademark, and exclusive license of Atlantyca S.p.A. All rights reserved. The moral right of the author has been asserted. Based on an original idea by Elisabetta Dami.

geronimostilton.com

Published by Scholastic Inc., *Publishers since 1920,* 557 Broadway, New York, NY 10012. SCHOLASTIC and associated logos are trademarks and/or registered trademarks of Scholastic Inc.

Stilton is the name of a famous English cheese. It is a registered trademark of the Stilton Cheese Makers' Association.

ISBN 978-0-545-10376-3

Text by Geronimo Stilton
Original title *Il Furto del Diamante Gigante*
Cover Art Director: Iacopo Bruno
Cover art by: Roberto Ronchi and Andrea Cavallini
Graphic Designer: Andrea Cavallini
Illustrations by WASABI! Studio (design) and Davide Turotti (color)
Graphics by Merenguita Gingermouse and Yuko Egusa

Special thanks to Katheryn Cristaldi
Translated by Julia Heim
Interior design by Kay Petronio

30 29 28 27 26   20 21 22 23 24

Printed in the U.S.A.   40
This edition first printing 2020

GO SQUEAKERS!

It was a very *special* evening. I left work at five on the dot and **RACED** home. I didn't even stop to smell the cheese at the All U Can Eat Cheese Palace! It was the night of the **big** soccer game, and my favorite team was playing—the **Cheddar Bay Kickers and Squeakers**.

Cheese niblets! Where are my manners?

Go Squeakers!

I almost forgot to introduce myself. My name is Stilton, *Geronimo Stilton*. I am the publisher of The Rodent's Gazette, the most popular newspaper on Mouse Island.

Anyway, where was I? Oh yes, I had just opened my front door when my phone *rang*. I glanced at the caller ID. It read **KORNELIUS VON KICKPAW**. I've known Kornelius since elementary school. Back then, he loved to protect me from the school **BULLIES**. And now he helps out mice all over the island. That's because he works as a real-life **SECRET AGENT**! His code name is **OOK**. Pretty impressive, I know.

"Hello, Kornelius," I said, picking up the phone. But the line went dead. Strange! I'd have to call my friend back after the game.

The soccer game was about to **START**. I quickly changed into my sweat suit with the

OOK

NAME: Kornelius von Kickpaw

CODE NAME: OOK

PROFESSION: Secret agent for the government of Mouse Island

WHO HE IS: Geronimo's friend from elementary school

ACCESSORIES: He always wears a super-accessorized tuxedo.

INTERESTING FACT: He always finds mysterious and bizarre ways to communicate because he doesn't want his messages getting intercepted.

Squeakers logo on it. Then I made myself a sandwich, cut a slice of cheese pie, and whipped up a **mozzarella milkshake**. Finally, I shut off:

 – **THE DOORBELL!**

– The phone!

 – **MY CELL PHONE!**

– **THE FAX MACHINE!**

 – **THE COMPUTER!**

Now **nothing** would disturb me. I switched on the television.

I was so **excited**. Even though I'm not much of a sportsmouse, I love the Squeakers.

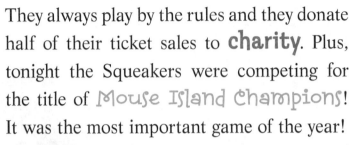

They always play by the rules and they donate half of their ticket sales to **charity**. Plus, tonight the Squeakers were competing for the title of Mouse Island Champions! It was the most important game of the year!

I settled into my favorite pawchair and turned up the volume. The two teams ran onto the field as music **PLAYED**. They lined up at center field and shook paws to show good sportsmouseship.

There were just a few minutes left before the opening *whistle*.

"COME ON, SQUEAKERS!" I cheered. I was so excited, I accidentally twisted my tail up in a knot. Youch!

While I was untwisting, I heard a terrible noise:

KERBANG!!!

I watched in **HORROR** as a giant steamroller blasted through my front door, **crushing** it to bits. Then it began to roll straight toward me!

"**HELP!**" I squeaked. What was happening? Why was some madmouse trying to flatten me like a pancake?

My fur stood on end. "P-p-please d-d-don't **HURT** m-m-me!" I cried.

Just then I heard a familiar snort. I stared hard at the mouse driving the steamroller. He had GRAY fur and a **SCOWL** on his face. I should have known. It was my crazy grandfather, **WILLIAM SHORTPAWS**.

One thing you should know about my grandfather: He doesn't like to be kept

waiting. Once we went to a FANCY restaurant and the service was terribly slow. Grandfather got so **angry**, he dumped a whole plate of creamy mashed potatoes over the waiter's head.

Now he stared at me with steely eyes.

"Geronimo, I have been trying to reach you for the past twenty minutes!" he shrieked, jumping off the steamroller. "I tried your phone, your **FAX**, and your **CELL**. I even rang your doorbell and **SCREAMED** in your window. How dare you not answer me!"

I gulped. "I was t-t-t-trying t-t-t-to watch the soccer g-g-game," I stammered. Did I mention I'm a tiny bit AFRAID of my grandfather? Well, okay, maybe I'm more than a *tiny* bit afraid — I'm a TOTAL scaredy-mouse!

Grandfather rolled his eyes. "SOCCER?!" he scoffed. "How many times do I have to tell you, Grandson? GOLF is where it's at!"

Ever since my grandfather retired and left me in charge of *The Rodent's Gazette*, he has *dedicated* himself to golf. He gets CRANKY if he doesn't play every day, and he insists on winning every match.

"Oh, before I forget, your friend Kornelius von Kickpaw called me. He's trying to reach you," Grandfather added. Then he grabbed my remote and dashed toward my television.

KORNELIUS again? I'd have to get back to him. But first I had to STOP my grandfather. He had plopped himself down in my pawchair and was *scarfing* down my cheese pie like he hadn't eaten in days. I tried my best to remain CALM until the

MOUSE ISLAND
RODENT GOLF ASSOCIATION
MEMBERSHIP CARD

FIRST NAME: William

LAST NAME: Shortpaws

NICKNAME: "Surestroke" Shortpaws

PERSONAL MOTTOS: "Squeak before you swing!" "Keep your paws on the ground and your snout to the wind!"

BRIEF PERSONAL STORY: He started playing way back when he was still drinking cheese from a bottle. His perfectly precise swing is the talk of the town. He has won more than fifty matches, twenty of which were on the RGA (Rodent Golf Association) Tour. He even won the New Mouse City Open in 2006. He is currently the president of the New Mouse City Golf Club.

unthinkable happened. Grandfather changed the CHANNEL.

"No!" I shrieked. "I'm watching the soccer game!"

But Grandfather didn't blink. A picture of a golf course appeared on the screen.

"Listen, Geronimo, my TV is on the fritz, so I'm using yours," he announced. "It's the **Furmax Masters Tournament**, and there's **NO WAY** I'm missing it. Case closed. End of story."

I chewed my whiskers to keep myself from screaming.

How could this be **HAPPENING**? I just had to see the game! I grabbed the phone and began dialing my friends. Nobody answered. They were all watching the game!

I tried the squeak & chew, the diner around the corner. They were closed. I thought about going to the office, but then I remembered Grandfather had **SOLD** the office television. He said the cable bill was too **EXPENSIVE**. I gnashed my teeth. I was going to miss the biggest game of the year, all because my grandfather was a **CHEAPSKATE**!

Then I had an idea. I could buy another television. I had always wanted one in my bedroom. I could fall asleep to my favorite reality show, **Cheese Boss**. With renewed hope, I called every last *electronics* store in town. But nobody answered. They were all watching the game!

Meanwhile, Grandfather was happily munching away, eyes glued to his **GOLF TOURNAMENT**. "Use the nine iron, you **furbrain**!" he shouted, **shaking** his paw at the TV.

I took off my glasses so I could cry freely. I felt like the only rodent alive stuck watching a **boring** golf game instead of the most **IMPORTANT** soccer match in Mouse Island history. It was **UNTHiNKABLE**! It was **UNIMAGINABLE**! It was **UNSQUEAKABLE**!

To make matters worse, the golf game didn't end until midnight.

By the time Grandfather left my house, I was **EXHAUSTED**.

I stared at the hole where my front door had once stood. Then I crawled into bed.

I fell asleep and dreamed I was being **attacked** by a crazed woodpecker. I woke up to a messenger pigeon *TAPPING* at my window. He held a note from **OOK**. It read:

"What kind of a nut wants to talk at **two** in the morning?" I grumbled. Then I went back to sleep.

WHAT A GAME!

The next day I got to my office super-early. I was still feeling down about missing the game, so I had decided to drown my sorrows by working. It wasn't easy. Everyone was talking about the **CHAMPIONSHIP**.

"Can you believe the Squeakers won?" my assistant, **Pinky Pick**, asked.

"What a game!" I heard in the kitchen.

To cheer myself up, I threw a breakfast party for the staff.

Oh, how I love a good pastry in the morning! I had a sip from my cup of hot cheddar, bit into a Danish, and smiled. It was filled with rich, creamy cheese and . . . a rolled-up piece of paper? Killer cat claws! What was a piece of paper doing in my Danish? It was another message from **OOK**.

Are you going to call me, or what? —OOK

I reached for the phone, but just then my grandfather charged into my office like a **TORNADO**.

"What's with all this partying, Grandson? Everyone, get back to work! **MOVE IT!**" he bellowed.

After the staff had left my office, Grandfather clapped his paws. "Enough wasting time!" he cried. "I've got **NEWS**! In a few days, the most important **GOLF TOURNAMENT** on Mouse Island is taking place in Mouseport. The winner gets to take home the *Super Mouse Cup*. It's made of solid **gold**, with a GIANT DIAMOND on top. I want you with me, Grandson. You'll be my **CADDIE**.*

I groaned. Isn't the caddie the one who carries the **HEAVY** golf clubs? My paws

*caddie: *Someone who carries golf equipment and acts as a technical consultant and strategist during a golf match.*

were sore just thinking about it. But of course, I agreed. I couldn't say **no** to Grandfather. He'd throw a **FIT**.

"Plus, I'll need you to keep your **EYES** peeled. Rumor has it one of the golfers is planning on **CHEATING**," Grandfather continued. He headed for the door, then turned back.

"Well, don't just stand there!" he shouted. "Our plane leaves in exactly **ONE HOUR**!"

I flew into a *panic*. One hour? I guess I could forget about finishing my cheese Danish. Oh, how I hate *rushing*!

No More Than
Two Pounds!

I ran home and **CRAMMED** my clothes into my suitcase. I was so rushed I forgot to call back **OOK**.

Just then the phone *rang*. It was Grandfather.

"Make sure you pack light," he squeaked. "And I mean really light, Grandson. No more than two pounds. Now move it! Move it! Move it!"

I repacked my stuff in a smaller bag, making sure I put in only the essentials. Then I *raced* to the airport.

Grandfather was nowhere in sight.

Suddenly, I heard someone calling me. I looked around, but all I saw was a huge **mountain** of luggage in the corner. Then a face popped out from behind it.

"Over here, Grandson!" my grandfather called.

I was **LIVID**. So that was why Grandfather wanted me to pack light! He wanted me to **CARRY** all of his stuff! I dragged everything to the check-in counter, where the ticket agent made us pay an expensive fee because the **luggage** weighed so much.

Over here, Grandson!

GRANDFATHER SHORTPAWS'S LUCKY CHARMS

LITTLE WOODEN OWL: BRINGS GRANDFATHER GOOD LUCK AND BRINGS BAD LUCK TO HIS ENEMIES.

PHOTO OF CHEESITA LOPEZ: SHE CONVINCED HIM TO LEARN TO PLAY GOLF.

A KEY CHAIN WITH THE NUMBER 18: IT WAS A GIFT FROM HIS UNCLE WHEN HE MADE HIS EIGHTEENTH HOLE IN ONE.

A PEELING AND YELLOWISH GOLF BALL

A SILVER CUP: THE FIRST CUP HE EVER WON.

PHOTO OF SHORTPAWS'S FIRST GOLF INSTRUCTOR

ANOTHER SILVER CUP: THE MOST RECENT CUP HE'S WON.

My back screamed in **PAiN**. Just then we heard an **ANNOUNCEMENT** over the loudsqueaker:

"MR. VON KICKPAW IS WAITING FOR MR. STILTON AT BOARDING GATE C12!"

Cheese niblets! It was **OOK**! I rushed to the boarding gate. Kornelius was hiding behind a newspaper.

"I **need** to tell you something **important**. . . ." he whispered.

But before he could continue, Grandfather dragged me away.

"No time for chitchatting, Grandson. My **FANS** are waiting. **WILLIAM SHORTPAWS, THE GOLF LEGEND**, cannot miss the plane!" he squeaked.

Grandfather pushed his way to the front of the boarding line. Two minutes later, we were in our seats. Grandfather took the window seat, which was fine with me. Did I mention I'm afraid of heights? After I checked my seat belt three times, we took off.

I should have known it wouldn't be an easy flight. Grandfather drove me CRAZY! ① First he insisted I ask the flight attendant for a glass of water with ice cubes shaped like golf balls. ② Then he wanted boiling hot coffee in his lucky mug. ③ And then he wanted the sports page of the newspaper! ④ Finally he ordered me to read a book called *The History of Golf for Dummies*. "I'll QUIZ you after the flight," he smirked.

I felt a **massive** headache coming on. What a trip!

INTRODUCTION TO GOLF

▶ THE HISTORY OF GOLF

Golf has uncertain origins. It first became popular in the 15th century in Scotland, where the courses at St. Andrews Links were established, then in all of Great Britain in the 18th century. The Royal and Ancient Golf Club, founded at St. Andrews in 1754, maintains the worldwide rules for the game.

▶ HOW TO PLAY GOLF

The player must hit a small ball into the assigned holes in order, using a club. A club has a long handle with a grip on one end and a weighted head on the other. The player uses clubs of different shapes and sizes depending on the situation. The goal is to get the ball in each hole by taking the smallest number of strokes, or hits, possible.

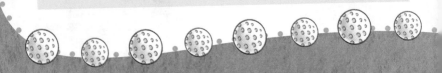

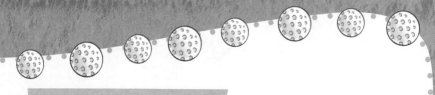

GOLF COURSES

In general, golf courses have 9 or 18 holes positioned at varying distances. The distance between each hole can vary between 328 to 1800 feet. Courses have different shapes and levels of difficulty. They may include "traps" such as sand pits, hills, and water to make it more challenging to get the ball in each hole.

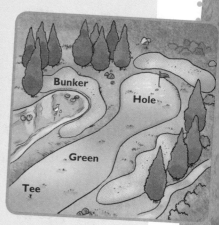

THE RULES OF GOLF

The first and most important rule of golf is that everyone is his or her own referee. Every mouse must be honest and respectful of the rules. Since each golf course is different, the characteristics of the course influence the rules.

WAKE UP!

When we finally reached Mouseport, I was so **TIRED** that I collapsed on the hotel bed and instantly fell asleep. I dreamed I was basking in the **SUN** at a luxurious tropical resort. Ah, it was so **RELAXING**, so **QUIET**, and so . . . **cold**?

I woke up to a blast of cold air in my snout. It was morning and my grandfather had flung open the window and was standing with his paws on his hips.

"**Wake up!**" he shrieked.

Oh, why does Grandfather have to be such a morning mouse? I **HATE** mornings!

Grandfather insisted I order a **ton** of food from room service. When the food didn't arrive within minutes, he made me call again.

"Tell them it's not just for *any* mouse. It's for **WILLIAM SHORTPAWS, THE GOLF LEGEND!**" he yelled.

When breakfast arrived, Grandfather made me call and complain. The coffee was not *hot* enough, the juice was too **tart**, and the morning newspaper was **crumpled**. Plus, he was convinced the knife and fork were from two different sets of silverware.

"**Unacceptable!**" Grandfather bellowed.

I was so busy complaining I almost didn't notice the note taped to the newspaper.

It read:

Call me already!!

—ook

I was about to call my friend, but Grandfather yanked the phone away. "No time!" he squeaked. **"WILLIAM SHORTPAWS, THE GOLF LEGEND**, cannot be *late* to the **GOLF COURSE**!"

We scampered downstairs and passed the front desk. That's when I heard everyone whispering, "That's him, *Geronimo Stilton*, the mouse who likes to complain about everything."

Those poor rodents on the golf course. I bet Grandfather would make me complain that the grass wasn't GREEN enough, the holes weren't DEEP enough, and the wind wasn't fresh enough!

I was so embarrassed I wanted to crawl into my **mouse hole** and never come out. But I couldn't. Not with Grandfather by my side.

"Get me a taxi, Grandson. And make sure you tell the driver to step on it!" he demanded.

"Now move it! Move it! Move it!"

NO TIP FOR YOU!

I hailed a cab and we took off. Grandfather complained the whole time. The seat belt was too **TIGHT**, the window was **DiRty**, and the ride was too **BUMPY**.

When we reached the **GOLF COURSE**, Grandfather bounded out of the cab and yelled at me to grab his bags. "That was the **worst** ride ever!" he squeaked at the driver. "No **TIP** for you!"

The driver fumed. Then he zoomed off, yelling, "I hope you play your **worst** game ever!"

We passed through the clubhouse, where the players get changed, then Grandfather led me to a back room. The first thing I noticed was all of the security equipment. There were VIDEO CAMERAS, infrared rays, and even MOTION SENSORS. The place was a rat burglar's nightmare! I was about to ask Grandfather what the security was for when I spotted the reason.

In the middle of the room stood a solid gold trophy that was bigger than the megahuge block of cheddar they sell at Squeaky's Wholesalers Club. At the top of the trophy was an unbelievably GIANT DIAMOND. The engraving on the trophy read: "*Super Mouse Cup of Mouseport Golf Tournament.*" I was in awe. *Super* wasn't the word for it. This thing was SPECTACULAR!

"The winners of the Mouseport Golf Tournament get to keep the cup for one year. Then they pass it on to the next winner," Grandfather explained.

The Super Mouse Cup, according to tradition, is given each year to the winner of the golf tournament. For the last ten years, the competition has been held in Mouseport.

The trophy looked like it weighed a TON. Not even my friend Bruce Hyena could have lifted it, and he's one STRONG mouse! I wondered how the winners got it home. Shipping it would cost a FORTUNE. And what if it was stolen on the way?

I was still thinking about the Super Mouse Cup when two of Grandfather's friends showed up. They were Arnold Pawmer and Clyde Clubfur. Arnold and Clyde were playing as a TEAM.

"Who are you playing with, William?" Arnold asked Grandfather.

Wilson Whitebelly

"I'm supposed to be playing with my old friend **Wilson Whitebelly**, but I don't understand why he's not here yet," Grandfather muttered, glancing at his **WATCH**.

Just then, Grandfather's cell phone **RANG**. He flipped open the phone, listened for a minute, then turned **pale** as a slice of provolone.

"**WHAT?!** You missed your flight?!!" he shrieked. "Now **WHO** am I supposed to play with?"

I could hear Wilson apologizing, but Grandfather wasn't listening. Instead he was staring at me with a **FIERY** look. One thing you should know about Grandfather—when he gets that look in his **EYES**, watch out!

"Grandson!" he squeaked. "You will take Wilson's place!"

I started to **PROTEST**. I hadn't played **GOLF** in years. But Grandfather didn't care. "As a young mouseling you were great, Grandson. You could have been a **champion** if you hadn't wasted your time reading books and watching silly soccer games," he squeaked. I tried to defend myself, but it was too late. Grandfather had made up his mind. Oh, how had I gotten myself into such a **mess**?

Psssst!

I left Grandfather and was headed for the clubhouse café when a paw stretched out from behind a column and tapped me on the shoulder.

"Psssssssssssssst!"

I jumped so HIGH, my head made a dent in the ceiling. Well, okay, maybe not that high, but you get the picture. Then I realized the paw was attached to my friend OOK, the SECRET AGENT.

"Geronimo, I have been trying to get ahold of you for twenty-four hours!" he hissed.

After explaining all about my ANNOYING grandfather, I said, "What did you need to tell me?"

My friend leaned in close. "I wanted to tell you to come to Mouseport, but lucky for me, you're already here! I'm on a SECRET MISSION for the government of Mouse Island. We have reason to believe one of the players is planning to steal the solid gold Super Mouse Cup with the world-famous GIANT DIAMOND!" he squeaked.

I was shocked. "And that's not all of it,"

OOK added. "The thief is planning on selling the diamond to **CAT PIRATES!**"

I gasped. "How unsqueakable!" I cried.

OOK nodded. "Exactly!" he agreed. "That's why I need your help. You **MUST** fill in for your grandfather's missing partner. That way, you can keep your eye on the players while I keep my eye on the *Super Mouse Cup*. If anyone tries to steal it . . . **BAM**, we'll catch him immediately. My sister, **Veronica**, was going to help me, but she fell off her high heels and twisted her ankle when she was working undercover."

OOK's sister is a secret agent, too. Do you know her? She is one beautiful rodent.

I tried explaining to Kornelius that I hadn't played **GOLF** in years.

OOV

NAME: Veronica von Kickpaw

CODE NAME: OOV

PROFESSION: Secret agent for the government of Mouse Island

WHO SHE IS: OOK's sister

DISTINGUISHING MARKS: She always wears a mysterious, delicate, and sophisticated perfume that makes her immediately identifiable and...fascinating!

INTERESTING FACT: She has a real passion for golf and for golf clothes and accessories. She searched all of the stores in New Mouse City to find her pink-striped, one-of-a-kind designer golf bag.

"I'll make a fool of myself," I whined. "All I remember about **GOLF** is that the ball is **round**."

Headlines flashed before my eyes:

STILTON STINKS UP SUPER MOUSE CUP TOURNAMENT

PUBLISHER LANDS HIGHEST SCORE* IN GOLF HISTORY!

Kornelius put his paw around me. "**COME ON**, Geronimo. I'm asking you in the name of *friendship* to do me this favor," he pleaded.

Of course, I had to agree. I never refuse a friend in need. Plus, there was one other reason I had to agree: My grandfather would KILL me if I didn't **PLAY**!

Now I had only one problem. I was still wearing my *suit*.

*In golf, the lowest score wins.

"I'll leave some clothes in the changing room," Kornelius said with a smirk. I wasn't sure what the smirk meant, but there was **no time** to figure it out.

I ran back to Grandfather to tell him I would play. He **grinned**. Then he began barking orders. I had to register, get dressed, and take a golf lesson.

"So you don't make me look **bad**," Grandfather explained.

I hustled to the players' changing room and found the clothes **OOK** had left for me.

But they didn't seem **quite right**.

That's when it hit me: The clothes belonged to OOK's **sister**!

First I put on Veronica von Kickpaw's pullover sweater. It was so **TIGHT** I could hardly breathe. Then I wriggled into her tiny pants and too-small golf shoes. **YOUCh!** Finally I plopped her green cap with the little pink heart on my head and picked up her small golf bag.

At that moment another player came into the changing room. He took one look at me and burst out laughing. I hadn't even hit the **GOLF COURSE** and I was already making a fool of myself!

Here are Veronica's clothes!

A SUPER-JAM-PACKED LESSON

I decided just to wear my own clothes. Then I rented some shoes and clubs and raced to the GOLF COURSE. Grandfather had hired me an instructor to give me a **super-jam-packed lesson**. A well-dressed mouse met me on the GREEN. "I am **Pendleton Putterat**," he said. "Are you ready for your **super-jam-packed lesson**?"

Before I could even squeak, Pendleton shoved a golf club at me.

"You have ten minutes to hit ONE HUNDRED BALLS. Go! Go! Go!" he shrieked.

When I finished hitting all of the balls, my muscles were killing me.

"Now you have ten minutes to do ONE

HUNDRED SQUATS," Pendleton told me. "**Go! Go! Go!**"

When I finished all of those squats I could barely walk.

"Now you have **ten minutes** to read this **HUNDRED-PAGE BOOK** about **GOLF** techniques," Pendleton said as he handed me the book. "**Go! Go! Go!**"

When I finished reading, my eyes were so bleary I could hardly see.

Pendleton slapped me on the back. "**GOOD LUCK!**" he said with a smirk. "You're really going to **need** it!"

I stumbled off. The tournament was about to begin.

At the first hole, I looked around for Grandfather. Suddenly, my fur turned the color of MOZZARELLA.

Standing a whisker's length in front of me

was **SALLY RATMOUSEN**! Do you know Sally? She is the **OBNOXIOUS** publisher of *The Daily Rat*, *The Rodent's Gazette*'s biggest competitor.

Then I realized Sally wasn't alone. Her grandmother was standing next to her! She's the one who founded *The Daily Rat* twenty years ago, when my grandfather started *The Rodent's Gazette*.

Just then my grandfather appeared. He **stomped** over to the Ratmousens and stuck out his paw. "May the best mouse win!" he announced. "But since I am **WILLIAM SHORTPAWS, THE GOLF LEGEND**," he muttered under his breath, "I think it will be us."

Sally's grandmother had thick glasses, a wart on her nose, and a snooty expression. "Well, I am **Molly Ratmousen, Lady Legend of Golf**, and I **KNOW** we will win!" she

MOUSE ISLAND
RODENT GOLF ASSOCIATION
MEMBERSHIP CARD

FIRST NAME: Sally

LAST NAME: Ratmousen

NICKNAME: Golf Tiger

PERSONAL MOTTOS:
"On the green, I'm the boss!"
"Careless caddies beware!"

BRIEF PERSONAL STORY:
Her grandmother taught her
everything she knows about golf. She's known
for breaking the rules, except on the golf course,
because that's unethical!

MOUSE ISLAND
RODENT GOLF ASSOCIATION
MEMBERSHIP CARD

FIRST NAME: Molly

LAST NAME: Ratmousen

NICKNAME: Lady Legend
of Golf

PERSONAL MOTTOS:
"Grandmas are golfers, too!"
"Don't judge a mouse by her
nine iron!"

BRIEF PERSONAL STORY:

Golf champion. She has competed in tournaments all
over Mouse Island and has won hundreds of trophies.
She has yet to win the Super Mouse Cup.

declared, glaring at us with **icy blue** eyes.

I gulped. **Molly Ratmousen** reminded me a lot of her granddaughter: **STRONG**, **tough**, and **SUPER CONFIDENT**. In fact, I was actually feeling a little bit frightened by the old mouse. Still, I didn't want to appear rude, so I stuck out my paw. After all, I am always a *gentlemouse*.

"Pleased to see you, madam," I began. "It will be a PLEASURE playing with you—"

But before I could finish, she ripped her paw from mine, smacking me in the snout with her enormous red ruby ring. SMACK!

"Listen closely, FURBRAIN," she commanded. "My granddaughter and I will win this tournament in the name of *The Daily Rat*! Now, hit the ball!"

Meanwhile, Grandfather pulled me aside. "I'm counting on you, Grandson, so don't mess this up. If you do, I'm taking back *The Rodent's Gazette*!" he threatened.

I felt another MASSIVE headache coming on.

OH FOR THE LOVE OF CHEESE,

how had I gotten myself into this mess?

MAP OF THE GOLF COURSE

1. Entrance
2. Parking lot
3. Reception
4. Pro Shop/Library
5. Driving range
6. Refreshment stand
7. Clubhouse
8. Restaurant/Café

HOLE #1

Before I hit my ball, I held it up for everyone to see. This way, no one would CONFUSE my ball with the others.

Molly stomped up to me. She ripped the ball from my paws and examined it closely.

How strange!

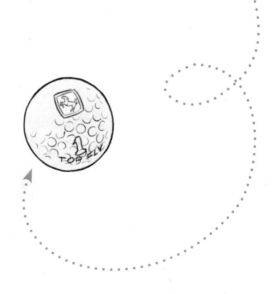

Finally, I hit the ball. Then Grandfather hit his ball and Sally hit hers. When it was Molly's turn, she swung **HARD**. But instead of heading for the GREEN, the ball flew straight at me! It hit me in the head!
BONKKKKKKKKKK!
I heard Sally's grandmother SQUEAK,

"Geronimo Stilton can't continue the match! Team *Rodent's Gazette* must forfeit!"

Then I fainted. Grandfather sprang up. "We are **NOT** forfeiting!" he yelled. "Bring me some water!" A mouse from the clubhouse came *RUNNING*. Grandfather poured freezing water over me. I woke up in a flash. My fur was **SOAKED**. My head

had a **lump**. And my knees felt **WEAK**.

"He's fine!" Grandfather insisted.

Molly giggled under her whiskers. How **strange**!

HOLE #2

At the second hole, my ball ended up in a **giant** tree. **Rats!**

Did I mention I'm **afraid** of heights?

MOLLY GIGGLED UNDER HER WHISKERS.

How strange!

HOLE #3

At the third hole, my ball ended up in the middle of a cactus patch. I had to play with a million **THORNS** pricking me in the fur. I felt like a walking pincushion. **Youch!**

"Do it for The Rodent's Gazette!" Grandfather ordered.

MOLLY GIGGLED UNDER HER WHISKERS.

How strange!

I wondered why. Did she hate me that much? She sure was one very unusual mouse!

HOLE #4

At the fourth hole, my ball ended up in a nest full of wasps. Wasps **BUZZED** all around me. When I hit the ball, they **ATTACKED**!

Oh, how had I gotten myself into such a **MESS**?

MOLLY GIGGLED UNDER HER WHISKERS.

How strange!

HOLE #5

At the fifth hole, my ball ended up in something called a bunker. It's a ditch filled with sand. Every time I hit the ball, I dug a **deeper** hole.

Soon I was covered up to my neck!

MOLLY GIGGLED UNDER HER WHISKERS.

How strange!

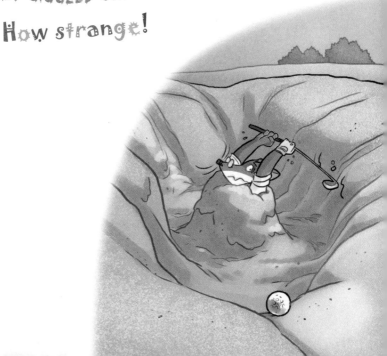

HOLE #6

At the sixth hole, my ball rolled off the golf course into a cow patty! When I swung . . .

spLASHHH!!!

Gobs of cow patty hit me. I smelled like a sewer rat. Everyone **RAN** away from me.

The only things sticking by me were the **flies**.

MOLLY GIGGLED UNDER HER WHISKERS.

How strange!

HOLE #7

At the seventh hole, no one could take it anymore. The wind was blowing my STENCH in the other players' direction. The Secretary of the golf association insisted that I wash off. Grandfather sprayed me down with a garden hose.

I had never been so humiliated in my **life**! Well, except for that time I sang onstage in just my underwear. But that's another story. . . .

MOLLY GIGGLED UNDER HER WHISKERS.

How strange!

HOLE #8

At the eighth hole, my ball landed in another tree, but this time it hit a bird's **nest**. The birds were not happy. One perched on my head and began **tweeting**. Oh, when would this **NIGHTMARE** end?!

MOLLY GIGGLED UNDER HER WHISKERS. How strange!

HOLE #9

At the ninth hole, Molly did something **shocking**. She offered me a delicious **HOT CHEDDAR** sandwich. I guess she felt guilty for laughing at me.

I polished off the sandwich in no time flat. Seconds later my stomach began to **gurgle**. Uh-oh! I made a mad dash for the bathroom.

How delicious!

But when I tried to leave the bathroom, I discovered that the door was **LOCKED**.

Someone had locked me in! It took TEN MINUTES to get me out of there. I was so **embarrassed**!

The other players were fuming. "You should be ashamed of yourself, Grandson. A **TRUE GOLFER** never keeps the other players waiting!" Grandfather scolded. I tried to explain, but he wouldn't listen.

"No excuses, Grandson," Grandfather barked. "Your behavior is UNSQUEAKABLE. Now get your fur in gear and hit that ball! **Move it! Move it! Move it!**"

MOLLY GIGGLED UNDER HER WHISKERS.

How strange!

HOLE #10

At the tenth hole, I hit my ball into a shrub, and it took forever to find it. **How embarrassing!**

MOLLY GIGGLED UNDER HER WHISKERS.

How strange!

HOLE #11

At the eleventh hole, I hit my ball into the **SAME** shrub. **What an odd coincidence!**

MOLLY GIGGLED UNDER HER WHISKERS.

How strange!

How strange!

How strange!

How strange!

HOLE #12

At the twelfth hole, my ball landed in the **same** shrub a third time! I couldn't believe my bad luck.

MOLLY GIGGLED UNDER HER WHISKERS.

How strange! How strange! How strange! How strange! How strange! How strange!

Hole #13

At the really unlucky thirteenth hole, my ball landed in a **muddy** swamp.

"**Go in after it!**" Grandfather insisted.

When I climbed out, I looked like a **SWAMP THING**. A frog even mistook me for a lily pad. My snout was **red** with embarrassment again, but I was so covered in **mud** that no one could **see** it!

MOLLY GIGGLED UNDER HER WHISKERS.

How strange!

HOLE #14

At the fourteenth hole, I calculated our score. Despite everything, we were playing well. But when I told Grandfather, he slapped a paw over my mouth. "You'll **JINX** us!" he hissed.

I didn't want to do that, so I said, "Actually, we're playing **TERRIBLY**."

Grandfather looked ready to **EXPLODE**. "Don't say that, either!" he shrieked.

I couldn't take it anymore. "So what **CAN** I say?" I asked.

"**Nothing!**" Grandfather thundered. "Be as quiet as a mouse!"

MOLLY GIGGLED UNDER HER WHISKERS. How strange!

HOLE #15

At the fifteenth hole, when I stuck my paw in the hole to get my ball, a *snake* popped out. "Ahhhh!" I yelled.

Luckily, the snake was rubber. I looked around to see who might be playing a prank. MOLLY GIGGLED UNDER HER WHISKERS. How strange!

HOLE #16

At the sixteenth hole, my ball was about to reach the hole, but then it made a **TURN**! It was as if my ball had a mind of its own!

MOLLY GIGGLED UNDER HER WHISKERS. How strange!

HOLE #17

At the seventeenth hole, a bush started CALLING to me. I tried to ignore it, but it was very persistent. Then I saw OOK waving from behind the bush. Thank goodness I wasn't going CUCKOO!

OOK had some big news. "**Molly Ratmousen** is cheating! She's using a remote-control ball. Watch her carefully," he whispered.

When it was Molly's turn, her ball landed far away from the hole. *So much for the "Lady Legend of Golf," I thought.* Then I noticed her **FUMBLiNG** with something in her pocket. Was she about to pull out another poisoned cheese sandwich? I backed away. No way was I going to fall for that trick again! Then I heard a loud buzzing sound. BUZZ!

Slowly, the ball began rolling toward the hole. It turned right, then left, then ZIGZAGGED its way straight into the hole.

OOK was right. **Molly Ratmousen** was cheating!

Bzz! Bzzzz! Bzzzzzz!

I wasn't shocked about Molly. After all, she was the grandmother of **SALLY RATMOUSEN**, who was my number one enemy. Sally **HATED** to lose. Once I was named *Publisher of the Year* and given an award onstage. Sally was so jealous she poured **glue** on my seat. When I stood up, my pants split **WIDE** open!

I was still thinking about **glue** when I heard **OOK** shriek in triumph. OOK had wrestled Molly's ball away from her and was holding it up to the **light**. The ball seemed perfectly normal. But then I noticed something strange. It was vibrating. Plus, it was making a funny buzzing sound: Bzz! Bzzz! Bzzz!

Next, **OOK** picked up my ball. "Just as I suspected!" he announced. At first I didn't know what he was *squeaking* about. What did he suspect? That my ball was perfectly fine and I was a lousy GOLFER? Then I heard it. **CHEESE NIBLETS!** My ball was *BUZZING*, too! But how?

OOK turned to Grandma Ratmousen. "Madam, I need you to empty your pockets," he said sternly.

Molly threw a fit. "**Get lost**, sonny!" she *SHRIEKED*. "I'm trying to play golf here!"

But Sally was **curious**. She insisted her grandmother do as she was told.

Reluctantly, Grandma Ratmousen pulled two **GADGETS** from her pocket. One had a **red** button with the initials **GS** on it. The second had a blue button with the

HAVE YOU FIGURED OUT MOLLY RATMOUSEN'S SECRET?

This was my original ball. . . .
Notice the number and the brand!

ULTRATOP BRAND

SERIES NO. 131313

This ball does not make buzzing
sounds and does not vibrate!

MOLLY WAS USING REMOTE-CONTROL-OPERATED BALLS!

This was the ball that had replaced mine. . . .

ULTRATRIK BRAND

SERIES NO. 83795648

This ball emits a buzzing sound!

initials **MR**. We all knew exactly what those initials stood for: *Geronimo Stilton* and **Molly Ratmousen**.

"Looks like someone's been controlling your ball, Geronimo," **OOK** said.

I have to admit, I was sort of happy. No, I wasn't happy that Molly had been

cheating. I was just happy that I wasn't such a **terrible** golfer! I mean, who hits their ball into a *SWAMP*, up two TREES, into a CACTUS PATCH, into a sand bunker, and into a wasp's nest all in one game?!

When everyone learned that Molly had been using remote controls, they were **disgusted**.

"You should be ashamed of yourself!" Grandfather scolded.

How Could You?

Even Sally looked completely floored. "But Grandmother, how could you do such a **terrible** thing?" she squeaked. "I know I've done some **rotten** things in my day, but never while I'm playing golf. The **GOLF COURSE** is a special place. We always play by the **RULES** here."

But Molly seemed unmoved. "Oh, shut your trap, you **NINCOMPOOP**. I don't give a rat's whisker about golf. I came here to steal the *Super Mouse Cup*!" she said.

Sally's jaw hit the ground. "But G-G-Grandmother . . ." she sputtered.

Molly just **rolled** her **EYES**. Then she did something astounding.

She pulled off her

RubbeR masK and stood up straight.

She removed her **FAKE TEETH**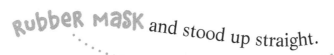

and **wig**.

And finally she threw her old-lady clothes into the air.

I **gasped**. The mouse wasn't Sally's grandmother, it was THE SHADOW! Do you know who the Shadow is? She's the most famous **THiEF** in New Mouse City!

The Shadow

NAME: The Shadow

LAST NAME: Ratmousen

WHO SHE IS: Sally Ratmousen's cousin

PROFESSION: The Shadow is the most notorious thief in New Mouse City. She is willing to do anything to get rich.

DISTINGUISHING MARKS: The Shadow is known for her clever disguises.

INTERESTING FACT: To disguise herself, she uses rubber masks, wigs, false teeth, and all different clothes. Underneath her disguises, she always wears a slinky black jumpsuit.

WHERE'S THE OLD LADY?

Before we could do anything, the Shadow took off toward a cluster of **PINE TREES** near the seventeenth hole.

Cheese niblets, she was fast!

OOK and I tried to follow her, but before we could reach her, she jumped aboard a **mini-helicopter** hidden between the trees. "Try to catch me, you fools!" she yelled as the helicopter **LIFTED** into the air. For some reason, I had a feeling the "fool" part was directed at me.

HOW INSULTING!

At that moment another thought **hit me**. If **THE SHADOW** had been **pretending** to be Molly Ratmousen, then where was Sally's **real** grandmother?

OOK seemed to have read my mind. "We need to find Sally's grandmother. She could be in *danger*," he said.

Then he added in a lower voice, "And remember, I need to talk to you later about something very, very SECRET."

I wondered what my friend wanted to talk about, but I didn't have time to think about it. We took off in separate directions.

"Grandma Ratmousen!" I called as I went.

Suddenly, I heard someone calling my name. I nearly jumped out of my fur when OOK popped his head out from behind a tree trunk. "One last thing. When you get back to the game, don't forget *they* are watching you," he said MYsterIOusLy.

Who were *they* and what did *they* want?

I wondered.

I hurried toward the clubhouse. When I got there, I looked in all the HIDDEN corners: under the stairway, in the BASEMENT, in the BATHROOMS, and in the changing rooms. The whole time I was yelling: "GRANDMOTHER RATMOUSEN! GRANDMA!"

When I passed in front of the door to one of the broom closets, I heard a strange muffled noise. Sure enough, when I pushed open the door, there she was. **Molly Ratmousen**!

She was *tied up* and gagged and looked very angry.

When I removed the gag, Grandma Ratmousen began

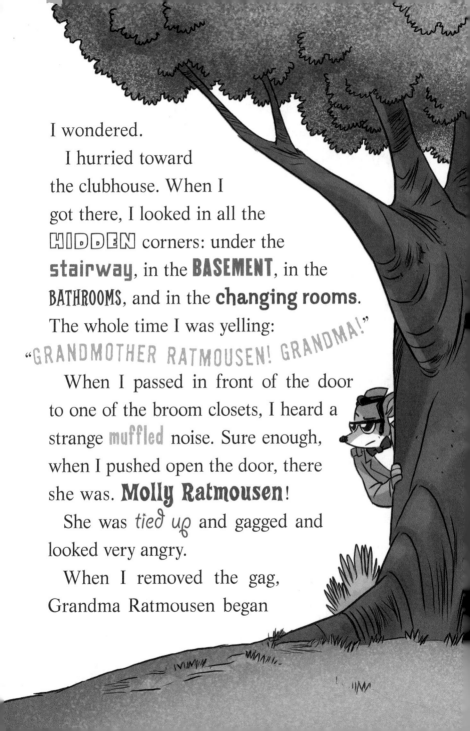

screaming at me. "Why didn't you save me earlier? You left me stuck in a broom closet for hours! You don't treat an **OLD LADY** this way! I had a very important match to win today. I was supposed to **defeat** William Shortpaws. Do you even know who I am? I am **Molly Ratmousen, Lady Legend of Golf**!" she shrieked.

I put my paw on her shoulder to **calm** her down.

"Everything's going to be okay now, Mrs. Ratmousen," I said in my **kindest** voice. "I am Geronimo Stilton and—"

But she didn't let me finish. "Young mouse, did you say *Geronimo Stilton*?" she cried.

I expected her to **thank me** for having saved her, so I repeated my name. "Yes, I am Stilton, *Geronimo Stilton*," I said.

"The **famouse** Stilton, the publisher

of *The Rodent's Gazette*?" she squeaked. "William Shortpaws's grandson?"

I nodded.

Then she **HIT** me over the head with her purse!

"Well then, take this, and this, and this!" she yelled.

HOLE #18

I tried to explain to Molly that it wasn't my fault that she had been **LOCKED** in the closet. Meanwhile I headed toward the eighteenth hole. Even after everything that had happened, Grandfather and I were still in the middle of the **TOURNAMENT**.

Luckily, when I reached the eighteenth hole, the judges were able to calm the old mouse down. They explained everything to her, including the Shadow's **trick**. Finally, Molly was **squeakless**. Thank goodness! Her high-pitched squeaking was making my fur **curl**!

"What took you so **long**, Grandson?" Grandfather complained. "Everyone's been waiting for you. I had to tell some **jokes** just to keep the crowd entertained."

I **GROANED**. Have you ever heard one of Grandfather's jokes? Let's just say they're the **OPPOSItE** of funny. I looked around at the crowd. **Holey cheese!** I couldn't believe how many of my friends and family were there. I saw my sister, THEA; **HeRCuLe PoiRat**, the famouse detective; my cousin **TRAP**; my nephew Benjamin; and the TV reporter Petunia Pretty Paws! I even spotted my cousin **Dino Stilton**, the great 𝒅𝒊𝒏𝒐𝒔𝒂𝒖𝒓 expert, who was just back from a long scientific expedition.

Then I looked at the GREEN and turned pale. My ball wasn't anywhere near the hole. Right at that moment a voice called out, "You can do it, Geronimo!"

Dino Stilton

I **blushed**. It was Petunia Pretty Paws. I've had a crush on her for the longest time, but whenever I'm around her, I turn into a **BUMBLING** fool. I started to trip over my own tail when I felt Grandfather's **STRONG** paw on my shoulder.

"Listen, Grandson, you've got to make this shot," he said. "If you do, we'll win the **TOURNAMENT**."

My heart **pounded**. "But my ball is so far from the hole," I whined.

Grandfather **stamped** his paw. "No excuses!" he squeaked. "I want to **win**!"

With trembling paws I gripped the golf club. I took a peek at the crowd. There were my friends and family, **cheering** me on. I couldn't let them down.

I took my best swing.

PING!

The ball ZIPPED through the air. As it approached the hole, I felt like my heart would **burst** right out of my fur. Did I do it? I couldn't **LOOK**.

Suddenly, everyone was screaming.

"Way to go, Grandson!" Grandfather shrieked. "WE WON!"

Petunia Pretty Paws ran up to me. "I'm so proud of you, G!" she cried, **kissing** me on the cheek. I would have thanked her, but I couldn't. I had already FAINTED.

A SECRET SURPRISE

After the game, there was a special celebration at the clubhouse. The president of the Rodent Golf Association presented us with the *Super Mouse Cup*. I stared at the GIANT DIAMOND glittering in the afternoon sun. It really was spectacular. I was glad I had been able to help Grandfather win it.

As I was admiring the cup, **OOK** POKED his head out from behind a column.

"**PSST!**" he whispered loudly. "Remember our meeting? **COME ON!**"

"Now?" I asked.

"Now," Kornelius said **seriously**. We **STEPPED** out into the hallway.

"Why did we have to leave the party?"

I asked Kornelius. "Do you *have* to be so **Mysterious**?"

My friend chuckled. "Better get used to it, Geronimo. I came to tell you that you passed the **TEST**!" he announced.

I scratched my head. I hadn't signed up for any test. "I don't know what you're talking about," I said.

But Kornelius kept babbling away. *"They have observed you and have declared you fit,"* he said. *"Congratulations,* Geronimo!" Then he gave me a **BONE-CRUSHING** hug.

"What are you **talking** about?" I squeaked.

"Wake up and smell the **CHEESE**," Kornelius said. "The heads of the Mouse Island Secret Service Organization (MISSO) have been watching you. They want you to become a **SECRET AGENT**. Isn't that fabumouse?"

So now I'm a **SECRET AGENT**. Just call me **00G**. So far I haven't had any cases like the GIANT DIAMOND ROBBERY. But when I do, I'll be sure to fill you in. **Mouse's honor!**

DO YOU KNOW HOW TO PLAY GOLF?

Now it's your turn: Can you play golf?
Choose the best answer for each question.
Mark your answers on a piece of paper.
Then, turn this page upside down and see if
you got the answers right. Good luck!

1 While another player is playing, you must:

a) be silent so as not to disturb her.
b) tickle her.
c) tell jokes to keep her happy.

2 How many holes can a golf course have?

a) four or twenty holes
b) nine or eighteen holes
c) seven or thirty-two holes

Answers: 1.a; 2.b; 3.a; 4.b; 5.a

3 In the game of golf:

a) Everyone is his own referee.
b) There is an official referee.
c) Everyone in the crowd watching acts as the referees.

4 In the game of golf:

a) There are no rules.
b) There are very specific rules.
c) It doesn't matter if you don't know the rules.

5 When and where was golf invented?

a) in Scotland in the 15th century
b) in France in the 20th century
c) in Italy in the 16th century

REMEMBER:

Everyone has different athletic skills that might make you prefer one sport over another. It doesn't matter what sport you choose as long as you like playing it!

Don't miss a single fabumouse adventure!

Up Next:

Visit Geronimo in every universe!

Spacemice

Geronimo Stiltonix and his crew are out of this world!

Cavemice

Geronimo Stiltonoot, an ancient ancestor, is friends with the dinosaurs in the Stone Age!

Micekings

Geronimo Stiltonord live amongst the dragons in the ancient far north!

Don't miss any of my adventures in the Kingdom of Fantasy!

THE KINGDOM OF FANTASY

THE QUEST FOR PARADISE:
THE RETURN TO THE KINGDOM OF FANTASY

THE AMAZING VOYAGE:
THE THIRD ADVENTURE IN THE KINGDOM OF FANTASY

THE DRAGON PROPHECY:
THE FOURTH ADVENTURE IN THE KINGDOM OF FANTASY

THE VOLCANO OF FIRE:
THE FIFTH ADVENTURE IN THE KINGDOM OF FANTASY

THE SEARCH FOR TREASURE:
THE SIXTH ADVENTURE IN THE KINGDOM OF FANTASY

THE ENCHANTED CHARMS:
THE SEVENTH ADVENTURE IN THE KINGDOM OF FANTASY

THE PHOENIX OF DESTINY:
AN EPIC KINGDOM OF FANTASY ADVENTURE

THE HOUR OF MAGIC:
THE EIGHTH ADVENTURE IN THE KINGDOM OF FANTASY

THE WIZARD'S WAND:
THE NINTH ADVENTURE IN THE KINGDOM OF FANTASY

THE SHIP OF SECRETS:
THE TENTH ADVENTURE IN THE KINGDOM OF FANTASY

THE DRAGON OF FORTUNE:
AN EPIC KINGDOM OF FANTASY ADVENTURE

THE GUARDIAN OF THE REALM:
THE ELEVENTH ADVENTURE IN THE KINGDOM OF FANTASY

THE ISLAND OF DRAGONS:
THE TWELFTH ADVENTURE IN THE KINGDOM OF FANTASY

THE BATTLE FOR THE CRYSTAL CASTLE:
THE THIRTEENTH ADVENTURE IN THE KINGDOM OF FANTASY

Don't miss the graphic novel by Geronimo and Tom Angleberger, artist and longtime fan!

The Sewer Rat Stink

A stinky smell is taking over New Mouse City! No mouse can live like this! Geronimo and his best friend Hercule, the private detective, head underground into the sewer world of Mouse Island to investigate. Can they save the city from the stench?

Don't miss any of my fabumouse special editions!

THE JOURNEY TO ATLANTIS

THE SECRET OF THE FAIRIES

THE SECRET OF THE SNOW

THE CLOUD CASTLE

THE TREASURE OF THE SEA

THE LAND OF FLOWERS

THE SECRET OF THE CRYSTAL FAIRIES

THE DANCE OF THE STAR FAIRIES

THE MAGIC OF THE MIRROR

Don't miss any of these exciting Thea Sisters adventures!

Thea Stilton and the
Dragon's Code

Thea Stilton and the
Mountain of Fire

Thea Stilton and the
Ghost of the Shipwreck

Thea Stilton and the
Secret City

Thea Stilton and the
Mystery in Paris

Thea Stilton and the
Cherry Blossom Adventure

Thea Stilton and the
Star Castaways

Thea Stilton: Big Trouble
in the Big Apple

Thea Stilton and the
Ice Treasure

Thea Stilton and the
Secret of the Old Castle

Thea Stilton and the
Blue Scarab Hunt

Thea Stilton and the
Prince's Emerald

Thea Stilton and the
Mystery on the Orient Express

Thea Stilton and the
Dancing Shadows

Thea Stilton and the
Legend of the Fire Flowers

Thea Stilton and the
Spanish Dance Mission

**Thea Stilton and the
Journey to the Lion's Den**

**Thea Stilton and the
Great Tulip Heist**

**Thea Stilton and the
Chocolate Sabotage**

**Thea Stilton and the
Missing Myth**

**Thea Stilton and the
Lost Letters**

**Thea Stilton and the
Tropical Treasure**

**Thea Stilton and the
Hollywood Hoax**

**Thea Stilton and the
Madagascar Madness**

**Thea Stilton and the
Frozen Fiasco**

**Thea Stilton and the
Venice Masquerade**

**Thea Stilton and the
Niagara Splash**

**Thea Stilton and the
Riddle of the Ruins**

**Thea Stilton and the
Phantom of the Orchestra**

**Thea Stilton and the
Black Forest Burglary**

**Thea Stilton and the
Race for the Gold**

**Thea Stilton and the
Rainforest Rescue**

Thea Stilton

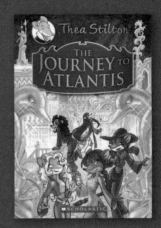

Secret Fairies

Don't miss any of these exciting series featuring the Thea Sisters!

Treasure Seekers

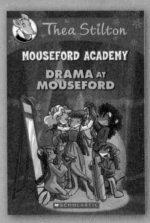

Mouseford Academy

1. Main entrance
2. Printing presses (where the books and newspaper are printed)
3. Accounts department
4. Editorial room (where the editors, illustrators, and designers work)
5. Geronimo Stilton's office
6. Helicopter landing pad

THE RODENT'S
GAZETTE

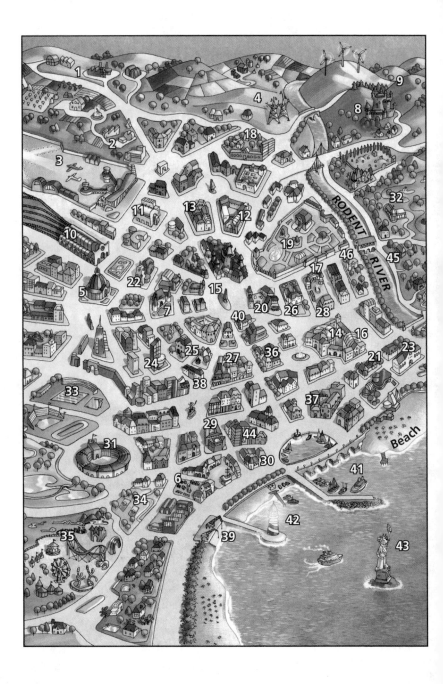

RODENT RIVER

Beach

Map of New Mouse City

Brigand's Isle

This way to the Rodent Straits

Tomcat Island

Pirate Ship
of Cats

Hamster Islands

Blue Dolphin
Bay

Coral Reefs

This way
to the Mousific
Ocean

Stray
Cat
Harbor

San Mouscisco

2

3

4

1

Cat's
Claw
Bay

Panther
Archipelago

Swissville

25

8

9

14

11

13

Cheddarton

12

10

23

Mouseport

32

15

21

22

This way
to the
Ratlantic Ocean

20

26

17

16

29

19

18

35

24

New Mouse City

Mousefort Beach

28

30

27

31

36

33

37

34

Furflung Island

N

W   E

S

MOUSE ISLAND

This way to the Sea of Mice

Map of Mouse Island

ABOUT THE AUTHOR

Born in New Mouse City, Mouse Island, **GERONIMO STILTON** is Rattus Emeritus of Mousomorphic Literature and of Neo-Ratonic Comparative Philosophy. For the past twenty years, he has been running *The Rodent's Gazette,* New Mouse City's most widely read daily newspaper.

Stilton was awarded the Ratitzer Prize for his scoops on *The Curse of the Cheese Pyramid* and *The Search for Sunken Treasure.* He has also received the Andersen 2000 Prize for Personality of the Year. One of his bestsellers won the 2002 eBook Award for world's best ratling's electronic book. His works have been published all over the globe.

In his spare time, Mr. Stilton collects antique cheese rinds and plays golf. But what he most enjoys is telling stories to his nephew Benjamin.